mary-kateandashley

TWO of a kind ™

It's Snow Problem

D0493657

Look for these

titles:

mary-kateandashley
TWO of a kind ™

It's Snow Problem

by Nancy Butcher

from the series created by Robert Griffard
& Howard Adler

TED SMART

A PARACHUTE PRESS BOOK

A PARACHUTE PRESS BOOK
Parachute Publishing, L.L.C.
156 Fifth Avenue
Suite 325
NEW YORK
NY 10010

This edition produced for The Book People Ltd,
Hall Wood Avenue,
Haydock, St Helens, WA11 9UL
First published in the USA by HarperEntertainment 2001
First published in Great Britain by HarperCollins*Entertainment* 2003
HarperCollins*Entertainment* is an imprint of HarperCollins*Publishers* Ltd,
77-85 Fulham Palace Road, Hammersmith, London W6 8JB

TWO OF A KIND characters, names and all related indicia are trademarks of
Warner Bros.™ & © 2000.
TWO OF A KIND books created and produced by
Parachute Publishing, L.C.C. in cooperation with Dualstar Publications,
a division of Dualstar Entertainment Group, Inc.

Cover photograph courtesy of Dualstar Entertainment Group, Inc. © 2001

The HarperCollins website address is
www.**fire**and**water**.com

ISBN 0 00 775042 0

Printed and bound in China

CHAPTER ONE

"I can't decide. Should I wear this sweater for the Winter Festival, or *this* sweater?"

Twelve-year-old Mary-Kate Burke glanced up from her desk. Her twin sister Ashley was standing in the doorway of her dorm. She held a fluffy pink cardigan in one hand and a black cashmere turtleneck in the other.

"I *do* look totally awesome in pink." Ashley held the cardigan up to her chest and struck a super-model pose. Then she did the same thing with the turtleneck. "But I look totally awesome in black, too. Hmm, major dilemma!"

Mary-Kate hit the SAVE key on her laptop and sighed. "Ashley, I know you're having a fashion emergency. But I'm in the middle of my own emergency, okay?" Mary-Kate had an English essay due in a day – and she hadn't written a sentence!

Ashley frowned at Mary-Kate's outfit. "Well, now that you mention it, that Chicago Bulls T-shirt *totally* doesn't go with those trousers."

"Hel-lo? That's not what I meant," Mary-Kate said. "Besides, why are you stressing out about what to wear for the Winter Festival? It's not for twelve more days!"

"It's never too early to start thinking outfits," Ashley replied. "Ashley's law. So have you decided which Winter Festival event you're going to sign up for?"

For a moment, Mary-Kate forgot about her homework troubles and got all excited thinking about the Winter Festival. The Festival was a competitive event between the White Oak Academy for Girls, which was their school, and the Harrington School for Boys, which was right down the road.

"Skating, I think," Mary-Kate said. "I've never done cross-country skiing, so that's totally out. I like downhill skiing and snowboarding a lot. But skating is my absolute favourite winter sport. Campbell is signing me up right now."

2

Campbell was Mary-Kate's roommate in Porter House – the coolest dorm at White Oak, in Mary-Kate's opinion.

"Why didn't you just go to the sign-up meeting yourself?" Ashley asked her.

Mary-Kate took a deep breath. "You know that English essay that's due tomorrow?"

Ashley nodded. "Yeah. On war themes in literature. I finished mine last night."

"Well, I kind of haven't," Mary-Kate admitted. "Finished mine, that is. *That's* the emergency I was talking about."

Mary-Kate hit a key on her computer, making her smiley-face screensaver vanish. Her English essay instantly appeared. All thirteen, incredibly brilliant words of it:

HOW THE TROJAN WAR BEGAN
ACCORDING TO HOMER'S *ILIAD*
BY MARY-KATE BURKE

Ashley walked over to Mary-Kate's desk and peered at the screen. "Huh. That's all you've got? Ms Bloomberg's going to have a total fit," she said.

I didn't really need to hear that, Mary-Kate thought.

"Ms Bloomberg is *not* going to have a total fit,"

3

she told her sister. "Because I'm going to get this essay done. Even if I have to stay up all night and skip dinner and breakfast and stuff."

Ashley leaned back on the bed. "Okay. Let's be practical here. We have to think of a good excuse for you to tell Ms Bloomberg."

Mary-Kate perked up. "A good excuse? Like what?"

"Like . . . hmm . . . you had an allergic reaction to your new Peaches 'n' Honey Shampoo, and you broke out in these yucky spots and you couldn't write because you were in total agony," Ashley suggested.

Mary-Kate shook her head. "Ms Bloomberg wouldn't believe me. I just saw her in the hallway about an hour ago, and I didn't have any yucky spots then." She sighed. "I think I'm just going to have to finish this paper by tomorrow morning."

"You can do it, Mary-Kate," Ashley said encouragingly. "I have faith in you!" She glanced at her watch, then jumped up from the bed. "Wow, it's almost three! The School Spirit Committee is starting in five minutes!"

"The who-what committee?" Mary-Kate asked her.

"The School Spirit Committee for the Winter

Festival. You know, to boost school spirit! I decided to sign up for that instead of one of the sports events." Ashley scooped up her pink and black sweaters and headed for the door. "See you later! I'll bring you some crisps from the vending machine!"

Mary-Kate waved goodbye to her sister. Then she turned back to her laptop.

Trojan War, Trojan War, Trojan War.

Mary-Kate knew the subject, no problem. She was just having a hard time putting pen to paper. Or, in this case, fingers to keyboard.

Just do it, she told herself. *Just type something . . . anything.*

The door opened and Campbell strolled in. She was wearing a Minnesota Twins jersey and faded jeans.

"Hey, Campbell," Mary-Kate called out.

"Hey, MK," Campbell replied. She sat down at her desk without looking at Mary-Kate.

"So. How did the meeting go?" Mary-Kate asked her.

Campbell shuffled through some papers, still not turning around. "Meeting?" she said blankly.

"The sign-up meeting for the Winter Festival," Mary-Kate reminded her. "You know! You were supposed to sign me up for the skating team." She frowned. "You *did* sign me up for the skating team, right?"

"W-ell . . ." Campbell hesitated.

Mary-Kate was getting a bad feeling in the pit of her stomach. "Campbell? What happened?"

"Um. Well. The skating team was full," Campbell explained. "And the cross-country-skiing team really needed some good people. So I kind of signed you up for that instead."

"*What?*" Mary-Kate gasped. "You can't! I mean, I don't know how to cross-country ski! You have to go back and un-sign me immediately!"

"It's kind of too late," Campbell told her. "We really need you there."

Mary-Kate's heart sank. Cross-country skiing was the one winter sport she knew nothing about.

I don't want to let Campbell down, she thought. *But I know if I join the cross-country team I'll make a total fool of myself – in front of the entire school!*

CHAPTER TWO

Ashley raced into the English classroom just as Ms Bloomberg was calling the School Spirit Committee meeting to order.

Getting to meetings on time should be a competitive event in the Winter Festival, Ashley thought. She tried to catch her breath.

Ms Bloomberg glanced up from her clipboard and smiled at her. "Hello, Ashley! Have a seat."

Ashley sat down in the front row and looked around. Her good friend Wendy Linden was there. So was her roommate, Phoebe Cahill.

This is going to be a great committee! Ashley thought happily.

"We're expecting a few more people, but we

might as well get started." Ms Bloomberg pushed her glasses up her nose and peered at her clipboard. "The purpose of the School Spirit Committee is to support the Winter Festival. If we get everyone really excited, then we'll have a big turnout at all the events."

"Do you mean like all the skiing and snowboarding races?" Phoebe asked her.

"There will be non-sports competitions, too," Ms Bloomberg explained. "Like the snow sculpture contest."

Snow sculptures! I could get into that! Ashley thought.

"Our purpose today is to decide how we should publicize the Festival," Ms Bloomberg went on.

Ashley waved her hand in the air. "We should do Winter Festival posters," she suggested.

"That would be great," Wendy agreed. "I can do some of the graphics on my computer."

"Wonderful, Wendy," Ms Bloomberg said, scribbling on her clipboard. "Posters are definitely the first step."

Just then, Dana Woletsky came sauntering into the room, followed by Summer Sorenson and her best friend Kristin Linquist. Dana was wearing a to-die-for outfit: great-fitting jeans and a black velour shirt.

Oh, no! Ashley thought, alarmed. *Does this mean Dana's on the committee?* She and Dana weren't exactly best friends. Dana had been out to get Ashley ever since she had accused Ashley of stealing her boyfriend, Ross Lambert. (Though according to Ross, he was never interested in Dana to begin with!) Now Ross was Ashley's sort of boyfriend – and Dana was still angry.

"Sorry we're late!" Dana said, her super-shiny black hair swinging behind her. "We were checking out the new 4-You music video on my big-screen TV."

"Just have a seat, girls," Ms Bloomberg said.

Dana narrowed her green eyes at Ashley, and sat down.

"We were just talking about ways to publicize the Winter Festival and boost morale," Ms Bloomberg explained. "Ashley suggested posters. Any other suggestions?"

Wendy raised her hand. "What about a pep rally?"

Dana leaned over and whispered something to Kristin. The two of them giggled.

"Great idea, Wendy," Ms Bloomberg said.

"We could show old documentaries about past Winter Olympics athletes at the pep rally!" Phoebe added, pushing her blue-rimmed cat-eye glasses up her nose. "That could be really inspiring! And, those athletes wore the coolest retro outfits. For example, I saw this '60s footage once . . . "

Phoebe was really into vintage clothes. Vintage, as in old. In fact, she was wearing black leggings under a faded velvet dress that looked practically ancient.

"'60s footage," Summer repeated blankly. "You mean like '60s shoes?"

"No, Summer, 'footage' means film clips," Ms Bloomberg explained.

Summer brushed a strand of blonde hair out of her eyes and blinked. "Oh," she said.

Ashley tried not to giggle. She liked Summer, but she really was an airhead sometimes.

Ashley was about to say something when she heard a sound in the doorway. She glanced up.

Standing in the hall, staring into the English classroom, were three boys. Three *Harrington* boys!

One of them was Ross Lambert, Ashley's crush. Ashley's heart fluttered at the sight of his seriously handsome face.

The other two were Jeremy Burke, Ashley and Mary-Kate's cousin, and Andrew Nunzio, one of the dreadful Nunzio twins. Arthur Nunzio was not with them.

Dana had spotted the boys, too. She jabbed one of her perfectly manicured fingernails in the direction of the doorway. "Spies!" she cried out. "Harrington spies!"

"We were looking for the Headmistress's office," Ross explained quickly. "Our Headmaster asked us to deliver a memo to her about the Winter Festival."

"It's in the Administration building," Ms Bloomberg told them. She gave them a funny look. "*This* is the English building."

"Okay, thank you," Ross said.

Before he turned to go, he smiled at Ashley and waved hi. Ashley smiled at him and waved back. Behind Ross's back, Jeremy stuck his finger in his mouth and pretended to throw up.

Typical gross Jeremy behaviour! Ashley thought.

After the boys left, Dana whirled around and stared at Ms Bloomberg. "Aren't you going to *report* them, Ms Bloomberg? Those boys were obviously spying on our School Spirit activities!"

Ms Bloomberg looked surprised. "Now, why would they do that, Dana?"

Dana flipped her hair over her shoulders. "You know Harrington's won the Winter Festival trophy for the last three years in a row. They'll do anything to make sure they win again!" She lowered her voice dramatically. "Anything," she whispered.

"I'm sure you exaggerate," Ms Bloomberg reassured Dana. She tapped her pen against her clipboard. "Okay, group, back to business. We've got posters . . . a pep rally . . . anything else?"

The committee brainstormed ideas for a while. Then Phoebe raised her hand.

"I know, I know!" she said excitedly. "How about official Winter Festival hats? I could design them, and all the White Oak students could wear them!"

"I think that's a terrific idea, Phoebe," Ms Bloomberg said enthusiastically. "Except – how will we pay for the materials to make the hats? This committee doesn't have much of a budget."

"How about a cake sale?" Ashley suggested. She was really into baking – cakes, biscuits whatever. If it was gooey or chocolaty or sugary, she was there!

"Really original idea," Dana muttered under her breath.

Ashley frowned at Dana. *Did she wake up on the wrong side of the bed this morning, or what?*

"A cake sale. Hmm, yes. That could work." Ms Bloomberg put her pen down and glanced up from her clipboard. "You know, we have a lot of work to do between now and the opening day of the Winter Festival, which is a week from Friday. What we need to do now is to assign a committee chairperson."

"I nominate Ashley Burke!" Phoebe said immediately.

Ashley smiled, surprised. "Wow, thanks, Phoebe," she said.

"I nominate Dana Woletsky!" Kristin spoke up.

Ashley's smiled faded. *Oh, no! Was this going to be a contest between her and Dana?*

"We have two nominations on the table," Ms Bloomberg declared. "We're going to need to take a vote. All in favour of Ashley?"

Phoebe and Wendy raised their hands.

"All in favour of Dana?" Ms Bloomberg added.

Kristin and Dana's hands shot up. Dana stared at Summer. After a second, she raised her hand, too.

"Dana, you can't vote for yourself," Ms Bloomberg told her. "That's two and two. A tie. Ashley and Dana, it looks like you're going to be co-chairs."

Co-chairs? Ashley's heart sank. *I have to work with Dana Woletsky?*

Ashley's eyes met Dana's. A satisfied-looking smile was spreading across Dana's face.

This could be trouble, Ashley thought. *I wonder if it's too late to un-nominate myself?*

CHAPTER THREE

"I hate the Winter Festival," Ashley moaned.

That's just what I was about to say! Mary-Kate thought.

It was Sunday night. Mary-Kate and her sister were sitting in the Porter House common room, munching crisps from the vending machine.

"*You* can't hate the Winter Festival, because *I* hate the Winter Festival," Mary-Kate told Ashley.

"*You* hate the Winter Festival?" Ashley said incredulously. "Since when?"

"Since Campbell signed me up for the cross-country-skiing team," Mary-Kate replied. "I've never cross-country skied in my life!"

"Well, you think that's bad?" Ashley countered.

"I have to co-chair the School Spirit Committee with Dana Woletsky! She never likes anyone's ideas except for her own. And she's so totally bossy – she'll try to run everything!"

Mary-Kate giggled. "Hey, Ashley! Remember when you used to want to be friends with her? Best friends?"

"Ancient history," Ashley muttered. "Hey, speaking of which! How's your Trojan War essay coming?"

Mary-Kate grinned. The words "Trojan War" didn't make her want to throw up any more.

"I made great progress after I saw you," she told Ashley. "I got four pages done! So now I have only one to go. I'm on the home stretch!"

"Excellent!" Ashley raised her hand in the air, and she and Mary-Kate exchanged high-fives.

Mary-Kate was about to pop another crisp in her mouth when she spotted Campbell poking her head into the common room.

Campbell smiled sheepishly at Mary-Kate. "Is it safe? Are you still cross with me?"

I could throw this crisp at her. Or I could be mature about it, Mary-Kate thought.

Let's go for mature. "No, I'm not cross with you, because you're going to find a way to get me off the cross-country-skiing team ASAP," Mary-Kate replied sweetly.

Campbell plopped down on the big, stuffed couch beside Mary-Kate. "MK, I told you. It's too late. Everyone's counting on you. Besides, you're looking at this all wrong."

"What do you mean, wrong?" Mary-Kate asked her.

Campbell folded her arms across her chest. "Okay. So you've never been cross-country skiing. It's a piece of cake! I could teach you in one or two easy lessons!"

"I don't think so," Mary-Kate said.

"Maybe Campbell's got a point," Ashley chimed in.

"Hey, whose twin sister are you, anyway?" Mary-Kate protested. "You're supposed to be on *my* side!"

"I *am* on your side, Mary-Kate," Ashley replied. "What Campbell is saying is, you're good at all sports. A warrior!"

A warrior! Mary-Kate liked that. "I guess so. True."

"And warriors don't back down from challenges," Ashley went on. "They also don't back down when their friends need them."

Mary-Kate sat up a little straighter. "That's true, too."

"Your friends need you, Mary-Kate!" Campbell chimed in. "The cross-country-skiing team needs you! White Oak Academy needs you!"

Mary-Kate sighed. "Oh, all right. I'll do it."

Campbell pumped her fist in the air. "Yes! So when do you want your first lesson?" she added. "How about tomorrow morning, before breakfast? There should be lots of fresh powder on the ground."

"If I get my Trojan War essay done tonight, I'll be there," Mary-Kate agreed.

Just then, Mary-Kate noticed Phoebe and Wendy standing in the doorway. They waved hi and came over.

"Hey, crisp time," Wendy said, plopping down beside Ashley.

Phoebe sat down on the arm of the couch. Mary-Kate thought she looked pretty cool in her 1950s vintage PJ set.

"I'm already working on some preliminary sketches for my Winter Festival hats," Phoebe announced. "I'm thinking that we can keep costs down by buying fleece hats in bulk and sewing designs on them." She turned to Ashley. "What do you think, Mademoiselle Chairperson?"

"You mean, Mademoiselle *Co*-Chairperson," Ashley corrected her. "I like your idea, but we'll have to run it by the other co-chairperson, too."

"You don't think Dana's going to kill all my hat ideas, do you, Ashley?" Phoebe said. She looked worried.

"Maybe we could lock Dana in a cupboard for the next twelve days," Wendy joked. "Better safe than sorry!"

"Maybe we could tell her the Winter Festival's been moved to Vermont," Mary-Kate added.

The five girls started giggling.

"Tell *who* the festival's been moved to Vermont?"

Mary-Kate's head shot up. *Uh-oh,* she thought.

Dana was standing in the doorway of the common room, hands on hips. Kristin was with her.

"Uh . . . no one, Dana," Ashley said quickly. "We were just, uh, brainstorming ideas for the Winter Festival."

Dana rolled her eyes. "Totally lame ideas, I'm sure. Listen, Ashley. As the *real* chair of the committee, I must tell you I am going to lead the School Spirit Campaign in a different, more radical direction."

"Huh?" Ashley started. "What are you talking about, Dana?"

"You'll see," Dana said mysteriously. She

cocked her head at Kristin. "Come on. There's nothing interesting going on here. Let's go over to my dorm and do pedicures. I've got Glitter Gold Flame."

"What is she *talking* about?" Ashley repeated to the others.

"I think Glitter Gold Flame is that new nail polish colour," Wendy offered.

"Not about the nail polish! I meant about the School Spirit Campaign!" Ashley said.

Mary-Kate shrugged. "Don't sweat it, Ashley. Dana's just talking big, as usual."

"I suppose so," Ashley said. But Mary-Kate could see that her sister wasn't convinced.

Monday morning was cold. No, not just cold. Freezing, frigid, polar-bear cold.

Mary-Kate wasn't sure what she was doing outside with Campbell, sliding around in the woods near the White Oak campus with long, skinny sticks stuck to her feet.

"C-can we go i-inside yet?" Mary-Kate asked Campbell, teeth chattering. She was having fantasies about breakfast in the warm dining hall. Warm oatmeal. Warm bacon and eggs. Warm *anything*.

"We're just getting started!" Campbell called out

cheerfully. "Okay, MK. This is called a telemark turn. Watch and learn from the master!"

Campbell dug her poles into the ground and skied a little way down the path. Then she bent down smoothly on one knee and turned to the right. A cloud of white, powdery snow rose up around her. As she came out of the turn, she went totally vertical again.

She stopped and glanced at Mary-Kate. "Go for it, MK."

"What? Me? You want me to do *that*?" Mary-Kate sputtered.

Campbell nodded. "Uh-huh. You can do it!"

Mary-Kate tried a couple of times. It was pretty hard at first, and she fell once or twice. But after half a dozen tries, she began to get the hang of it.

In fact, an hour and many practice runs later, Mary-Kate was thinking: *I've totally nailed this cross-country-skiing thing! Well, maybe not nailed it, exactly. But it's not as bad as I thought!*

Actually, it was kind of fun. Mary-Kate liked pushing through the deep, powdery snow using only the sheer, brute strength of her arms and legs. It was like a combination of skating, which she loved, and downhill skiing.

"You're doing great, MK!" Campbell called out

when they were swooshing down a gentle hill.

"I am a pro!" Mary-Kate shouted as she executed a near-perfect telemark turn.

"You are a pro!" Campbell echoed.

"I am a warrior!"

"You are a warrior!"

Just then, a tree appeared in Mary-Kate's line of vision. It was straight ahead of her, and she was about to plough into it. "I am . . . *toast!*" she shouted.

She had no idea what to do. Instinctively, she slammed her poles into the ground, hard. She jolted to an abrupt stop and then fell headfirst into a pile of snow.

Splat!

Mary-Kate heard giggling behind her. Brushing the snow out of her face, she glanced up and glared at Campbell. "You didn't tell me what to do about trees," she complained.

Campbell offered a hand to hoist Mary-Kate up. "That was going to be my *next* lesson," she said. "Avoiding Trees 101."

Mary-Kate stood up and shook the snow out of her hair. It was definitely time for a warm breakfast *something* in the dining hall!

"Listen, Campbell, can we call it a day?" Mary-Kate pleaded. "I'm kind of . . ."

Then she heard the sound of voices in the distance. She stopped talking and looked around.

About thirty yards away, three guys were cross-country skiing through the woods. Three Harrington guys: Ross Lambert and that guy Skip from biology and a blond guy she didn't recognize. They were singing some sort of song that sounded like an army chant. And they were going really, really fast.

The competition, Mary-Kate thought grimly.

"I've changed my mind," she said to Campbell. "Let's do a couple more runs!"

CHAPTER
FOUR

Ashley hugged her books to her chest and headed down the hall to her English lesson. Her head was spinning with ideas for the School Spirit Committee. Posters, hats, the pep rally, the cake sale – and that was just the beginning!

Dana or no Dana, I'm going to be the most dedicated co-chairperson the committee has ever seen! Ashley thought.

Then Ashley stopped in her tracks.

A bunch of girls were gathered round the display case in the front hall, whispering.

What's going on? Ashley wondered.

Ashley edged to the front of the crowd, where Wendy and Phoebe were standing. "Hey, what's going on?" Ashley asked them.

Phoebe pointed to the display case. "Look!"

Ashley looked.

Something was definitely *wrong*.

The last time the White Oak girls had won the Winter Festival trophy was four years ago. Harrington had won each year since then.

White Oak's Winter Festival trophy from four years ago was always displayed in the centre of the display case.

Always – until now. Because the trophy was kind of not there. As in, gone.

And in its place was a toy stuffed squirrel.

"Ohmigosh," Ashley gasped.

The squirrel was the White Oak mascot, just as the ram was the Harrington mascot. Except this squirrel didn't look like the usual mascot at all. Its fur was mangy and ragged-looking. And it had a fake cast on its leg!

"Who do you suppose is responsible for this caper?" Phoebe was saying to Wendy.

"I don't know," Wendy replied. "You have to admit, it's kind of funny."

A shrill voice rose above the excited buzzing of the crowd. "It was Harrington!" Dana cried out. "Harrington did this! This means war!"

A couple of other girls raised their fists and shouted: "Yes!"

War? Ashley stared at Dana. Wasn't that going a little overboard?

"We must mobilize!" Dana exclaimed.

More fists went up in the air. Dana marched off, followed by a bunch of girls. They looked as though they were going off to . . . well, battle.

Ashley stared after them. *Why is Dana overreacting like this?* she wondered. *And where is the White Oak trophy?*

"Did everyone finish their essays on war themes in literature?" Ms Bloomberg asked the class.

Ashley glanced over at her sister and raised one eyebrow. Mary-Kate pulled her essay out of her backpack and grinned. Ashley gave her a thumb's up and mouthed the words: *Way to go!*

"I believe I'll have a few of you read your essay out loud to the class," Ms Bloomberg announced.

There were groans all round. Ms Bloomberg pushed her glasses up her nose and began scanning the room. Everyone slunk down in their seats.

Ashley slunk, too. *The trick with slinking is to do it in a really cool, subtle way,* she thought. *That way, it isn't so obvious to the teacher.*

Ms Bloomberg's eyes fell on Ashley – and stayed there. Ashley froze. *My slinking skills must be off today,* she thought anxiously.

Then Ms Bloomberg's eyes moved on. "Mary-Kate Burke!" she said brightly. "Why don't you come up to the front of the class and read your essay?"

Ashley sighed with relief, then shot Mary-Kate a sympathetic look. Mary-Kate shrugged.

Mary-Kate rose from her seat and walked up to the front of the room. She cleared her throat and began to read.

"How the Trojan War Began, According to Homer's *Iliad*," Mary-Kate said. "The Trojan War was a mythical war between the Greeks and the Trojans. An ancient Greek writer named Homer wrote about it in an epic poem called *The Iliad*.

"It all started as a love story. Paris, the son of King Priam and Queen Hecuba, fell in love with the beautiful Helen of Sparta. She fell in love with Paris, too. The problem was, she was already married to King Menelaus of Greece.

"While King Menelaus was away, Paris and Helen ran off to Troy. When King Menelaus found out, he decided to wage war against the Trojans."

"Bummer," one of the girls in the class muttered. Someone else giggled.

Ashley started to giggle too, but put her hand over her mouth. *Better not interrupt Mary-Kate*, she thought.

"Um, the war raged for ten years," Mary-Kate went on. "The Greeks couldn't get inside the gates of Troy. Then, one day, they came up with a plan. They built a huge wooden horse and left it outside the gates of Troy. One of the Trojans told the Greeks that the Trojans had given up, and that the horse was a gift.

"The Trojans were really psyched, and they let the horse in through the gates. The thing was, lots of Greek soldiers were hiding in the belly of the horse. So while the Trojans were sleeping, the Greek soldiers came out and killed the Trojan king and lots of other Trojans, too. They set Troy on fire. So finally, the Greeks won . . ."

Mary-Kate went on to talk about what happened after the war. When she finished reading, she glanced up. Ashley saw that Ms Bloomberg was beaming at her.

"Wonderful, Mary-Kate!" Ms Bloomberg said. "Excellent essay! Now, who's next?"

While Fiona Ferris was reading her paper, Ashley heard the sound of whispering behind her. It was Dana.

"This stuff about the Trojan War is giving me an idea," Dana said to Kristin. "I know just how to get those Harrington guys!"

Ashley frowned. Had Dana totally lost it?

Was she planning to build a huge Trojan horse to take to the gates of Harrington?

CHAPTER FIVE

"Okay, MK – go, go, *go!*"

It's my turn! Mary-Kate thought nervously.

Mary-Kate braced herself as Campbell came skiing down the path through the woods. The second the two girls were side by side, Mary-Kate took off.

It was after school on Monday, and the cross-country-skiing relay team was practising together for the first time. Campbell was number three on the team. Mary-Kate was number four – the all-important anchor!

Mary-Kate took off through the woods. *Okay, what did Campbell teach me this morning? Glide, pole, glide. Keep the knees bent and loose. And look out for trees!*

She skied through the dense woods, kicking up glistening clouds of snow as she moved. *This cross-country-skiing thing is definitely not bad*, she thought happily.

The route took Mary-Kate on a circular path through the woods. When she reached the end, her team-mates were waiting for her. Some girls from the other Winter Festival teams were watching, too. Everyone cheered as she crossed the finishing line.

Mary-Kate executed a telemark turn, then came to a stop with a big, snowy *whoosh*.

"Way to go, MK!" Campbell exclaimed, clapping her on the back.

"Thanks!" Mary-Kate said, panting. She was completely out of breath.

"You're a natural athlete, Mary-Kate," Lexy Martin told her. "Have you thought about joining the downhill team? We could use your talents!"

Wow, that's so nice! Mary-Kate thought. "Thanks, that would be really cool!" she said to Lexy. "But I think I need to concentrate on cross-country. You know, one team at a time."

"Well, think about it," Lexy said. "We've got an opening."

Lexy took off towards the downhill skiing area. Mary-Kate was about to say something to

Campbell when Fiona Ferris came up to her. She had a graffiti-painted snowboard tucked under one arm.

"You were really cool out there, Mary-Kate!" Fiona said enthusiastically. "Have you thought about joining the snowboarding team? We have one opening left!"

Wow, everyone loves me today! Mary-Kate thought.

She smiled at Fiona. "Thanks, Fiona. But, you know, I'm already on the cross-country team. And I don't want to overdo it."

"That's okay," Fiona said. "But let us know if you change your mind." She waved goodbye and took off to join her other team-mates.

Campbell turned to Mary-Kate. "Gosh, you're popular!"

"I suppose so," Mary-Kate said. She felt really flattered that everyone was paying so much attention to her. She'd always been in the limelight in softball and basketball. But it was a new thing to be noticed for her winter sports talents – which she didn't even know she had until this morning!

Lisa Dunmead came up to the two girls. "Hey, Mary-Kate. You looked great out there! Listen, I heard you wanted to be on the skating team. And we've just got an opening – Charlotte Atherton had to drop out because she sprained her ankle."

"Great!" Mary-Kate said. "I mean, not great about Charlotte's ankle. But great about the opening!"

"Well, how about it?" Lisa asked her.

Mary-Kate hesitated. *Skating is definitely my favourite winter sport*, she thought. *And it's the team I wanted to be on to begin with.*

But now that I'm on the cross-country-skiing team, I'm kind of into it!

"I think I'll need to say no," Mary-Kate said to Lisa after a moment. "I want to focus on cross-country."

"Well, let me know if you change your mind," Lisa said.

Campbell took off her ski gloves and blew into her hands. "Huh. My feelings are seriously hurt. Nobody asked *me* if I wanted to be on their teams."

"I suppose you're not an amazing, awesome super-athlete like me," Mary-Kate joked.

Campbell looked kind of hurt. "Thanks a lot."

"Campbell, I was just kidding!" Mary-Kate said quickly. "I wouldn't even know how to cross-country ski if it weren't for you!"

Campbell broke into a grin. "And don't you forget it!"

"No way! When I win my first Olympic medal for cross-country skiing, I'm going to mention you in my speech. 'I'd like to thank all the little people, like my First Form personal coach Campbell Smith . . . '" Mary-Kate teased.

Campbell giggled and whacked Mary-Kate with her ski gloves. Mary-Kate scooped up a pile of snow and squished it into Campbell's parka.

"Okay, enough, enough!" Campbell said, laughing. "Practice is over for the day, anyway. I have to get back to the dorm. We'll do this again tomorrow."

Campbell started skiing towards the school. Mary-Kate was about to follow her, then changed her mind. *My telemark turn needs more work*, she thought.

"You coming?" Campbell called over her shoulder.

"I think I'll stay out here and practise a little bit more on my own," Mary-Kate told her.

Campbell waved and took off. Mary-Kate stared up at the grey-blue sky. The light was starting to fade. She would stay out here for half an hour, tops – then grab some hot chocolate!

Just then, there was a *whoosh*ing noise, and a big, powdery cloud of snow blasted her in the face.

Yuck!

"Ugh! What was *that*?" she cried out.

She wiped the snow out of her eyes with the back of her mitten and blinked. Someone was standing in front of her.

A boy. A really *cute* boy.

He was tall and muscular, with golden-blond hair, big blue eyes, and fantastic cheekbones. He looked like a cross between a Gap model and Brad Pitt.

"Uh . . . hi," Mary-Kate managed to say when she remembered how to speak English. Then she realized that this boy was the reason she'd been blasted in the face with snow. "Aren't you going to, um, apologize?" she asked him.

"For what?" the boy said, sounding irritated.

"For kicking snow in my face," Mary-Kate said.

"I was in the zone." He shrugged. "I was concentrating on my poling technique. I am in training for the Harrington Winter Festival."

"Oh, you go to Harrington?" Mary-Kate said. She noticed that he still hadn't apologized for blasting her with snow. "Are you new there? What's your name?"

The boy tossed his head back, which kind of messed up his perfect golden-blond hair. In a cute way. "I just started last week. My name is Hans Jensen."

34

Mary-Kate introduced herself. "So you're on the cross-country-skiing team for Harrington?"

"I am on *all* of the teams for Harrington," Hans replied.

Huh? What was this guy talking about? Mary-Kate wondered. "*All* of the teams?" she repeated.

Hans looked her up and down as if she were a really annoying insect. "I am the best downhill skier, best cross-country skier, best snowboarder, and best skater at Harrington. So of course I am on all four teams I plan to lead Harrington to its fourth straight trophy!"

Mary-Kate tried not to burst out laughing. Hans was so full of himself!

Hans smirked at her. "And you? I don't suppose you're on any of the White Beech teams?"

"White *Oak*!" Mary-Kate corrected him huffily. How dare he assume that she wasn't on any of the teams! "As a matter of fact, I'm on . . . all four teams, too!" she blurted out.

Mary-Kate clapped her hand over her mouth. What did she just say?

Hans looked at her in surprise. "You are on all four teams?" he asked her. "I wouldn't have expected that."

"Why not?" Mary-Kate snapped. "You're not the

only super-athlete in this town. I'll see you a week from Friday – and I expect to lead White Oak to victory!"

"We'll see about that!" Hans snapped back.

The two of them skied off in opposite directions.

Mary-Kate stabbed her poles into the snow extra-hard as she skied. She was furious at the arrogant Hans. She'd show him who was the best athlete around. She'd show him—

Oh, no! What have I done? she asked herself.

Mary-Kate gulped. She had just told Hans she was on all four teams!

That meant she would have to say yes to Lexy, yes to Fiona and yes to Lisa. She'd have to join their teams after all.

It also meant she would not sleep for the next eleven days and just train, train, train.

Who needs sleep, anyway? Mary-Kate thought.

CHAPTER SIX

"Whoever stole the Winter Festival trophy from the main display case must come forward immediately," Mrs Pritchard announced.

It was Tuesday morning. Ashley and all the White Oak girls were sitting in the school hall for Mrs Pritchard's Morning Announcements.

Next to Ashley, Mary-Kate was yawning for what seemed like the hundredth time. *Why is she so sleepy?* Ashley wondered.

"I know that pranks have sometimes been part of the pre-Winter Festival ritual," Mrs Pritchard went on. She frowned. "But I absolutely will not tolerate the theft of the trophy."

Dana was sitting a few rows in front of Ashley

and Mary-Kate. Ashley saw her raise her hand.

Mrs Pritchard pointed to her. "Yes, Dana?"

"Why do you assume it was one of us, Mrs Pritchard?" Dana spoke up. "It was obviously one of those Harrington students!"

"It is possible that some of the boys were responsible," Mrs Pritchard agreed. "I have taken this up with the Harrington headmaster. He is addressing his students this morning, as we speak."

She added, "Either way, whoever is responsible, I want that trophy returned. I hope that is crystal-clear."

"Yes, Mrs Pritchard," all the girls said in unison.

"Thank you for your attention," Mrs Pritchard said. She peered over the rim of her glasses at her notes. "The oatmeal flavour of the day will be . . . banana-pecan."

Ashley jumped up from her seat. All the other girls did, too. This was Ashley's favourite part of Mrs P's Morning Announcements: the part where she announced the breakfast oatmeal flavour. It was her special way of saying: assembly dismissed!

Ashley turned to her sister. "I've got to go meet Phoebe in the dining hall. We have to talk to Dana about some School Spirit Committee stuff."

Mary-Kate just yawned and waved goodbye.

Once in the dining hall, Ashley found Phoebe right away. The two of them got some banana-pecan oatmeal and headed over to Dana's table.

Dana was sitting with Kristin and Summer. She glanced up when she saw Ashley and Phoebe and gestured towards some empty chairs. "Please have a seat," she said sweetly. "To what do we owe this pleasure?"

"Phoebe has some hat sketches to show us," Ashley said, sitting down. "And I want to go over some of Wendy's poster ideas, too. Plus, we need to nail down dates for the pep rally and the cake sale."

Phoebe took some sketches out of her backpack and laid them out on the table.

"My plan is, keep it simple," Phoebe began. "Especially since we don't have that much time, and we don't know how much money we'll be able to raise at the cake sale. There are some really cool-looking fleece ski caps on sale at the mall. I thought we could buy them for all the students and then add this design. Here, see what you think!"

Ashley peered over Phoebe's shoulder at her sketches. There was a drawing of a simple green fleece ski cap. There was another drawing of a little squirrel. It was wearing earmuffs and a muffler and skates.

It was totally adorable! "Wow, that is so cute!" Ashley told Phoebe.

"We can scan this design into a computer and get iron-on patches made from it," Phoebe explained to the group.

Dana rolled her eyes and didn't say anything. Ashley and Phoebe exchanged a glance. *What's up with her?* Ashley wondered.

She reached into her backpack and pulled out Wendy's poster ideas.

"What do you think of these, Dana?" Ashley asked her. "Wendy came up with six poster concepts. Here's one that says, 'WHITE OAK RULES!' And here's another one that says, 'WHITE OAK WELCOMES YOU TO WINTER FESTIVAL!' with a picture of this cute little snowman."

"Snowperson," Phoebe corrected her.

"Snowperson," Ashley said quickly. "And here's another one that says—"

Dana shook her head, making her dark hair flop back and forth. "No, no, no, *no*. You two are missing the point!"

"Huh?" Ashley and Phoebe said together.

"I believe that the entire School Spirit campaign should be based on the spirit of the Trojan War," Dana explained. "Forget about fuzzy hats and snowmen, snowpeople, whatever. Think blood! Think betrayal! Think battle!"

Dana slammed her fist on the table, making everyone jump up.

"This is a battle between White Oak and Harrington!" Dana cried out. "They've beaten us three years in a row. They sneaked through our gates during the night and stole our trophy. And now we must fight back!"

Kristin banged her fist on the table. "Yeah!"

Summer looked confused, but banged her fist on the table, too. "Yeah!" she repeated, then stared at her hand. "Oops, I broke a nail."

"I want to see tougher posters, with an edge," Dana demanded. "And these hats. They're too cutesy. I want a battle motif!"

Ashley stared at Dana. "Dana, you can't be serious. The School Spirit campaign should be upbeat and positive. You can't want something really negative."

"I'm overruling you on this, Burke," Dana said simply.

"You can't overrule me, we're co-chairs!" Ashley insisted.

"I say I'm right, and I'm overruling you," Dana repeated.

*   *   *

Ashley was still stewing over her conversation with Dana later that morning. She and Mary-Kate were taking the shuttle bus to Harrington school for their history lesson.

"What do you mean, Dana overruled you?" Mary-Kate asked Ashley.

"Dana didn't overrule me. She tried to. We just couldn't agree on anything," Ashley complained. She tried to keep her voice low, since Dana was sitting just a few rows behind them.

"Wow, forget White Oak versus Harrington," Mary-Kate remarked. "It's more like Ashley Burke versus Dana Woletsky!" The shuttle hit a bump. "*Ow!*" she cried out, rubbing her shoulder.

Ashley glanced at her sister, concerned. "What's the matter with you?"

"I'm in pain," Mary-Kate admitted. "I got up at five a.m. this morning so I could practise cross-country, downhill, snowboarding and skating. My muscles hurt. *All* my muscles, including my brain. And I'm totally exhausted!"

"*Why* did you sign up for all four teams?" Ashley asked her. "I mean, isn't that kind of insane?"

"Long story," Mary-Kate mumbled. "And don't worry. I'm not a quitter! I'm a warrior!"

My sister has totally lost her mind, Ashley thought.

The shuttle took a right turn, and Harrington school came into sight. Like White Oak school, it was made up of several big, pretty buildings all covered with ivy.

"Everyone's starting to think that somebody from Harrington stole the trophy," Ashley told her sister. "I guess pranks are a big part of the Winter Festival tradition. You know, Harrington pulls a prank on White Oak, then White Oak retaliates, and so on . . ."

"Huh. Does that mean *we're* supposed to pull a prank on them next?" Mary-Kate said.

Ashley was about to reply when she noticed something out the window. Something not quite right. *Uh-oh*, she thought.

"Maybe we already did," Ashley said slowly.

She pointed to the Harrington "Welcome" sign, which was posted just outside the school gates. Usually it said:

Welcome to Harrington
Home of the Winning Rams

But not any more. Someone had painted over the sign with bright red paint. Now it read:

Two of a Kind

Welcome to Harrington
Home of the LOSER RATs

And in the bottom right-hand corner of the sign was a picture of a little rat!

CHAPTER SEVEN

"The Wars of the Roses were very important in English history," Mr Yoshida told the class. He turned around and started writing dates on the blackboard.

A paper aeroplane went whizzing by Mary-Kate's nose.

Huh? What? she thought, dropping her pen.

She glanced around, trying to figure out who the culprit was.

She saw the Nunzio twins, Arthur and Andrew, across the room. They were whispering to each other and giggling about something. Behind them was her new arch-nemesis, Hans Jensen. He was paying careful attention to Mr Yoshida's lecture and taking lots of notes in his notebook with an expensive-looking silver pen.

Was Hans the paper aeroplane thrower? Mary-Kate wondered. That didn't seem like his style.

Then she noticed cousin Jeremy smirking at her from two aisles over. Mary-Kate made a face at Jeremy and mouthed the words: *Cut it out!* She picked up the paper aeroplane and made a point of ripping it into shreds while Jeremy was watching.

"Mary-Kate Burke, may I ask what you are doing?"

Uh-oh! Caught! Mary-Kate thought. Mr Yoshida was glaring at her, his arms crossed over his chest.

"Uh, sorry. Nervous habit." Mary-Kate stopped ripping and quickly folded her hands in her lap.

Mr Yoshida frowned at her and turned back to the blackboard again. "And no bubble gum in class, Ms Smith!" he said without turning around.

From across the aisle, Mary-Kate saw Campbell quickly extract a gigantic purple wad from her mouth.

Mr Yoshida continued talking about the Wars of the Roses. Mary-Kate tried to concentrate, but it was difficult. She couldn't stop thinking about her sore muscles. She also couldn't stop thinking about all the practices she had to attend after school. Picking up her pen, she scribbled in her notebook:

1455 – the Wars of the Roses start
2:45 – cross-country skiing
3:30 – downhill
4:15 – snowboarding
5:00 – skating
5:45 – pass out and die!!!!!!!

Mary-Kate sighed and shook her head. *I am not a quitter*, she told herself. *I am a warrior!* She glanced over at Hans, and felt doubly determined.

As soon as the history lesson was over, Ashley rushed up to her and grabbed her arm, hard.

Mary-Kate flinched. Everything hurt! "Ow! Watch it! I have snowboarding-elbow," Mary-Kate complained.

"Never mind that," Ashley hissed. "I have a theory. I think Jeremy took the trophy!"

Mary-Kate stared at her sister. "Huh? Why?"

"Think about all the pranks he's pulled in the past," Ashley reminded her. "Plus, he kept looking at me all through the lesson like he knew something."

"Let's go talk to him," Mary-Kate suggested.

Jeremy was hanging out in the hall outside Mr Yoshida's classroom. He grinned when he saw the twins. "Hi, ladies! Isn't it a fine morning?"

"Jeremy, do you know anything about the missing trophy?" Mary-Kate demanded. "Like, where it is?"

"Trophy? What trophy?" Jeremy said innocently.

"The Winter Festival trophy," Ashley told him.

"Oh, *that* trophy!" Jeremy said loudly. "You didn't tell me it was *that* trophy." He shrugged. "Sure, I know where it is. *Not!*"

The Nunzio twins passed by at that moment. "Maybe a squirrel took off with it!" Arthur called over his shoulder.

Andrew started cracking up. Some of the other boys in the hallway began to laugh, too.

"That's real mature," Ashley muttered.

Just then, Mary-Kate caught sight of Hans Jensen leaving Mr Yoshida's classroom, his nose buried in his history textbook. "I'll be right back," she said to her sister.

Mary-Kate walked up to Hans. "Hey, Hans," she said cheerfully. "How are your workouts going?"

Hans glanced up from his history textbook and gave Mary-Kate a condescending smile. "Excellent. I skied the Pinewood Trail this morning in eight minutes flat!"

"Oh, really?" Mary-Kate said sweetly. "I did that run, too. In seven minutes forty-five seconds."

Okay, so maybe it was more like eight minutes forty-five seconds. But he didn't need to know that.

"Seven . . . forty-five?" Hans repeated. He looked alarmed.

"Uh-huh," Mary-Kate said, nodding.

"I'm late for class," Hans said, and took off abruptly.

Mary-Kate rubbed her hands together gleefully. *I'll get you yet, Hans Jensen!* she thought.

"I am so dying for pizza," Mary-Kate announced.

She, Ashley, Wendy and Phoebe were hanging out in the common room. Mary-Kate had survived hours of killer practice sessions and had collapsed at five forty-five p.m., as per schedule.

But she was never too tired for pizza!

Mrs Pritchard had pizzas delivered to all the dorms every Tuesday night. Of all the White Oak traditions, this was definitely one of Mary-Kate's faves!

But Ashley wasn't interested in talking about pizza. She was still obsessed about Jeremy and the missing trophy.

"Jeremy was definitely looking seriously guilty in history today," Ashley said. "I really think he took the trophy."

"I just can't believe that Jeremy is related to you two," Wendy said to the twins, shaking her head. "He must be like a genetic mutation, or something."

Or something, Mary-Kate thought. "What about Andrew and Arthur Nunzio? They were acting kind of weird in class, too."

"They *are* weird. That wasn't acting," Phoebe pointed out.

The four girls proceeded to discuss the sign-painting incident. "I bet Dana and her friends did that," Ashley concluded. "I was watching her on the shuttle, after we all spotted the sign. She didn't act surprised at all!"

"That makes the score Harrington, one, White Oak, one. We're tied," Mary-Kate said. "And it's Harrington's turn to bat. I wonder what they'll do next?"

Just then, the pizza delivery man appeared in the doorway. He had a pile of pizza boxes in his arms

Mary-Kate jumped up to get one of the boxes for her, Ashley, Wendy and Phoebe. She sat down on the rug and opened the box.

"Yum!" she said. Then she did a double take. "I mean, *yuck!* What is *that*?"

Instead of pepperoni and sausage, the pizza was all covered with – acorns!

50

CHAPTER EIGHT

"Acorns?"

Ashley couldn't believe her eyes. There were acorns all over their big, yummy pizza.

Acorns, as in oak trees – as in White Oak Academy!

"Harrington!" Ashley exclaimed. "The boys did this!"

Other girls in the student lounge were yelling about acorns, too. It turned out that all the pizzas the guy had delivered had acorns sprinkled on them.

Thinking quickly, Ashley jumped to her feet and rushed into the hall. She wanted to see if the pizza man was still there. But he was nowhere in sight.

When she got back to where Mary-Kate and the

others were sitting, Wendy was saying, "Harrington Two, White Oak One!"

"Yeah," Ashley said worriedly. "I wonder what Dana and her friends are going to do to get back at them."

Phoebe pushed her glasses up her nose. "Girls, we have to be sensible about this and not get caught up in all the madness," she pointed out. "It's important that we stay focused on our work for the School Spirit Committee. And those of us who are competing in the athletic events need to stay focused on our training."

Ashley was impressed by Phoebe's attitude. "That is so true," she said. "Thank you, Phoebe!"

"I think we should focus on what's *really* important here," Mary-Kate suggested, pointing to the pizza. "Let's get rid of these acorns, so we can eat!"

"What do you think?" Ashley said to Phoebe and Wendy.

She pointed to a poster that read:

WHITE OAK ACADEMY FOR GIRLS
WELCOMES YOU TO
OUR WINTER FESTIVAL!

It was Wednesday after school. The three girls had got up really early that morning to make lots of posters. Now they were busy putting them up in the main hallway and elsewhere.

"I am so glad we decided to try out Phoebe's squirrel design for both the hats *and* the posters," Ashley said. "The squirrel looks so cute with its earmuffs and muffler and skates!"

"I agree," Wendy said, nodding. "What does your co-chairperson think of our posters?"

Ashley shrugged. "I'm not sure. I emailed Dana last night and told her that the three of us were going to make some sample posters and put them up in the hall, and that she could decide if she liked them or not. But she didn't write back."

"Typical," Wendy muttered.

"Well, *I* think the posters look fabulous!" Phoebe crooned. "The typeface and colours are very 1970s! Thank you, Wendy, for all your sophisticated computer work!"

The three girls continued down the hall, taping up more posters. When they'd finished with the main hallway, they turned the corner to start on the side hallway.

"Oh no!" Ashley exclaimed.

There were already several posters on the walls

of the side hallway. But these were definitely not the squirrel posters.

Ashley rushed up to the closest poster. It had a picture of a boy lying unconscious on the ground, with a pair of wrecked skis next to him. He had a sweater with a big H on it. A girl wearing a sweater with the letters WO stood over him with her foot on his chest. She was waving her ski poles in the air victoriously.

The poster said:

WHITE OAK VERSUS HARRINGTON
BATTLE TO THE DEATH
NEXT FRIDAY
BE THERE!

The other posters were variations on the war theme. Ashley could see them up and down the side hallway.

"Dana's been here," Ashley hissed. "I *knew* I shouldn't have emailed her last night to tell her what we were doing! She and her friends must have had an emergency poster-making session!"

"These posters are terrible!" Phoebe exclaimed. "The colours are all wrong, and the typeface is inconsistent with the mood of the graphic . . ."

"Who cares about that? These posters are just nasty and mean," Wendy declared.

"We've got to find Dana and talk to her," Ashley said. "Come on!"

She headed back round the corner to the main hallway.

"*Oh no!*" she exclaimed again.

All the squirrel posters were gone. In their place were more of Dana's posters!

Dana strikes again! Ashley thought, getting really angry now.

Just then, she spotted Dana way down the hall. Summer and Kristin were with her. They were carrying boxes of rolled-up posters – her posters!

"Dana!" Ashley called out. "Hey!"

Dana and her friends turned the corner and disappeared from view.

Ashley took off running after them. She was about to turn the corner, too, when she ran smack into – Mrs Pritchard!

"What are you doing, Ashley Burke? No running in the halls!" the Head snapped, straightening her glasses.

"I'm sorry, Mrs Pritchard," Ashley apologized immediately. She glanced over her shoulder. Wendy and Phoebe were right behind her, looking sheepish. "It's just that we really, really needed to talk to Dana right away . . ."

"Perhaps that can wait. I just received some very disturbing news," Mrs Pritchard said gravely.

Ashley stared at the Head. She did seem pretty disturbed about *something*. Something more than slamming into Ashley in the hall.

"Perhaps you girls are familiar with Gomez the Goat," Mrs Pritchard went on.

"Gomez the Goat?" Wendy said, looking totally confused.

"The Harrington mascot," Mrs Pritchard explained.

"I thought they were the Harrington *Rats*," Phoebe said. "I mean, *Rams*."

"They *are* the Rams. They just, er, couldn't find a ram, so they had to settle for a goat. And pretend that it was a ram. *Anyway*." Mrs Pritchard cleared her throat. "That's not the point. The point is, I've just received a call from the headmaster at Harrington. Gomez is missing!"

"What!" Ashley cried out.

"That's not all. Apparently some Harrington boys saw a group of girls lurking suspiciously about the Harrington premises this morning.

Possibly *White Oak girls*," Mrs Pritchard repeated, staring meaningfully at Ashley, Phoebe and Wendy.

Ashley, Phoebe and Wendy all looked at each other. "W-we don't know anything about a goat or a ram or anything," Ashley sputtered to Mrs Pritchard.

The Head sighed. "Look. I understand about these pre-Winter Festival pranks. Why, when I was your age . . ." She blushed and shook her head. "The point is, this latest prank takes the goat. Takes the biscuit, I mean! The Harrington Headmaster has told me that unless Gomez is returned, the Winter Festival may have to be cancelled!"

CHAPTER NINE

Mary-Kate could barely walk.

She was making her way down the hall of Porter House, trying to put one foot in front of the other. Her legs felt as though they were made of jelly. Or oatmeal. Really overcooked oatmeal.

This is what happens when you're a warrior, Mary-Kate told herself with a sigh.

She had spent the last three hours doing some serious cross-training in all four of her sports. On the bright side, her times had been really, really good. She was beginning to feel like she could pull off this multiple-team-thing after all.

On the not-so-bright side, she felt like sleeping for the next two weeks.

Mary-Kate reached her door and turned the knob. *I can't wait to get into my warm, cosy bed,* she thought. *I'm going to peel off my sweaty tracksuit, get into my flannel pyjamas and crawl under my duvet. And dream about total and complete victory over Harrington.*

She went inside and set her backpack down on the floor.

"Ba-a-a-a-a!"

Mary-Kate jumped. "Huh? Campbell, is that you? Do you have a cold or something?"

"Ba-a-a-a-a!"

It was a really weird sound. It didn't even sound human. Where was it coming from?

And then Mary-Kate saw. Standing at her desk, munching on what looked like her notes from history class, was a goat!

A *goat*?

Mary-Kate clapped her mouth over her mouth to keep from screaming. What was a *goat* doing in her room?

Maybe I'm imagining this, she told herself. *Maybe I've just been working out too hard. I should go over to the school nurse and get checked out or something.*

"Ba-a-a-a-a!"

Mary-Kate stared at the goat. No, she definitely wasn't imagining it.

The goat was black with white spots, two little horns and really bizarre eyes. They were round and yellowish, with thin black horizontal slits for pupils.

Actually, it's kind of cute, Mary-Kate thought.

The goat fixed its strange eyes on Mary-Kate. And then it started chomping up some more of her history notes.

"Hey! Stop that!" Mary-Kate yelled. She rushed across the room and grabbed the history notes out of the goat's mouth. The goat had really strong jaws, though. It wouldn't give up the notes.

"Let go, you crazy goat! Let go, or I'll . . . I'll—" Mary-Kate pulled on the notes extra-hard. They ripped in half. The other half was still in the goat's mouth.

The goat stared innocently at Mary-Kate, chewed, and swallowed. *Gulp!*

Mary-Kate wagged a finger at the goat. "Goat, you're in serious trouble now! You just ate the first half of the Wars of the Roses!"

"So *you're* the goat thief!"

Mary-Kate whirled around. Mrs Pritchard was standing in the doorway. She looked kind of upset.

"The goat thief?" Mary-Kate said blankly. "Huh? I just found this goat in my room. It was pigging out on my history notes. Who does it belong to?"

"There's no need to pretend, Mary-Kate," Mrs Pritchard said, sighing heavily. "I'm disappointed in you. And I'm afraid I must set an example for the rest of the school. It's the only way to stop these pranks and to keep them from getting out of control."

Mary-Kate was totally confused now. "Set an example? What are you talking about, Mrs Pritchard?"

"I'm afraid I can't let you participate in the Winter Festival," Mrs Pritchard declared.

"W-what?" Mary-Kate cried out.

No Winter Festival! she thought. *This is the worst thing that has ever happened to me!*

CHAPTER TEN

Ashley sat cross-legged on her bed, putting the finishing touches on her care package for Mary-Kate.

Let's see . . . the latest issue of Sports Illustrated. *Six protein bars. Six cans of protein shake, assorted flavours. A bottle of strawberry body glitter. And some extra-special macadamia-nut brownies baked by me!*

Ashley tucked everything into a pretty basket lined with a red-and-white napkin. Then she tied a red ribbon on the handle of the basket.

Sighing, she got up to deliver the package to Mary-Kate.

My poor sister, Ashley thought.

It was obvious to Ashley. Somebody else had

stolen Gomez and decided to frame Mary-Kate for the crime!

The question is, who? she wondered.

Five days had passed since Mrs P found Gomez in Mary-Kate's room. Five long, long days. And during those five days, Ashley had taken it upon herself to find the real thief and clear her sister's name.

The problem was, even if she managed to do that in time for the Winter Festival, it might already be too late.

Mary-Kate hasn't been able to practise with any of her teams for the last five days, Ashley thought. *The Winter Festival starts on Friday, just four days from now. Even if I find the thief today, there's no way Mary-Kate can be ready for cross-country, downhill, snowboarding and skating by then!*

Ashley sighed again. *This is not good*, she thought.

She soon reached Mary-Kate's door, and knocked.

"Enter!" her sister's voice called.

Ashley went inside. She didn't see Mary-Kate anywhere. "Mary-Kate? Where are you?"

"Down here!"

Ashley looked down. Mary-Kate was lying on

the floor, her arms out in a T position. She was holding her history textbook in one hand and her English textbook in the other and lifting them in the air in a circle. Up, down, up, down . . .

"*What* are you *doing*?" Ashley demanded.

"Lifting weights," Mary-Kate explained breathlessly. "Six sets of twelve chest flies. Then I'm going to do bicep curls and tricep kick-backs and ab crunches." She added, "These books are great! They're about five pounds each, which is perfect!"

Ashley plopped down on Mary-Kate's bed. "Why are you doing this?"

"Just because I can't practise with my teams doesn't mean I can't stay in shape," Mary-Kate answered. She set the textbooks down with a loud thump. "I have to be ready to compete, in case you find the goat thief by Friday. *Have* you found the goat thief?" she added hopefully.

Ashley hesitated before answering. She wished more than anything that she had some good news for Mary-Kate. But she didn't. "No. My number one suspect is still Dana, though."

Mary-Kate sat up a little. "She's still not talking?"

Ashley shook her head. "No, but she's still on her big campaign to 'get' Harrington. Plus, wouldn't it be just like Dana to kill two goats . . . I mean, birds . . . with one stone?"

"What do you mean?" Mary-Kate asked her.

"I mean, by stealing Gomez, she gets Harrington," Ashley explained. "And by framing you, she gets one of us. I found out that Mrs P came to your room last Wednesday because she got some sort of anonymous tip that Gomez was in your room."

"Anonymous, as in 'Dana Anonymous Woletsky'," Mary-Kate grumbled. "This is so unfair! I was totally framed! I had nothing to do with the goat-napping!"

Ashley grabbed her sister's shoulders and squeezed them, hard. "I know. But we'll beat this thing – together."

Mary-Kate bit her lip and nodded.

Ashley knew how her sister felt. She was really upset about the whole thing, too. But they couldn't fall apart now. They had to hang in there, catch the thief, and make sure Mary-Kate could compete in the Winter Festival!

Ashley pushed the basket towards Mary-Kate. Mary-Kate's face lit up. "Hey, what's this?"

"Care package," Ashley explained.

Mary-Kate dug through the contents. "The latest

Sports Illustrated! And protein bars! And – oh, wow! Your home-made macadamia-nut brownies!"

Mary-Kate reached over and gave Ashley a big bear hug.

"Thanks, Ashley," Mary-Kate said softly. "For the basket, I mean."

"Hey, what are twins for?" Ashley said with a shrug.

Mary-Kate sniffed. Then she took a brownie, split it in two, and offered half to Ashley. "So. What's new with you?"

Ashley munched down on her brownie half. "What's new. Hmm. Oh, the usual insanity. The pep rally's going to be on Thursday. All the Winter Festival hats are done. We've got several of these green fleece caps at the shopping centre, on sale. Phoebe, Wendy and I spent the weekend putting squirrel patches on them. They look pretty cool!"

"Did Dana help?" Mary-Kate asked her.

Ashley shook her head. "No, in fact, she wanted a totally different look for the hats. Some sort of warrior design. But almost everyone else liked Phoebe's squirrel design instead."

"*That's* a relief," Mary-Kate said.

Ashley grabbed another brownie. "And then, of course, the cake sale is tomorrow. We've been baking like mad all day. I hope we make lots of money!"

"Well, just bake lots of these, and you'll be rich!" Mary-Kate said, popping another brownie into her mouth. She sighed. "I feel so out of it! All this stuff is going on – the cake sale, the pep rally, everyone gearing up for the Winter Festival. And I'm not going to be able to participate!"

Mary-Kate looked upset all over again. Ashley was about to lean over and give her another hug. But then she noticed something.

On the floor near where Mary-Kate had been doing her weird exercises was a crumpled-up piece of paper.

Ashley leaned over to pick it up. "What's this?" she asked Mary-Kate.

Mary-Kate glanced at it and shrugged. "Oh, it's probably one of Campbell's failed three-point shots."

"Oh." Ashley unfolded the paper. It was a piece of stationery bordered by black stars, asteroids, and space ships. In the middle of the page, in purple Magic Marker, was written: PORTER 12.

What does that mean? Ashley wondered. *Was it some kind of code?*

Ashley showed the piece of paper to Mary-Kate. "Did you write this?"

Mary-Kate stared at the piece of paper and frowned. "Uh, no, I don't think so. I don't recognize that stationery, either."

"Porter Twelve, Porter Twelve," Ashley muttered. And then it came to her, like a lightning bolt. "Porter Twelve! Mary-Kate! That's your room number!"

"Oh, yeah," Mary-Kate said, nodding.

"This was written by someone who wanted to find your room," Ashley explained. "As in, someone who wanted to find your room and leave a goat in it!"

"We've found the goat thief!" Mary-Kate screamed and grabbed Ashley's shoulders.

"Ow, you're hurting me," Ashley complained. "We haven't found the goat thief yet!"

But already, Ashley's mental wheels were spinning. She had a plan. Sort of. And if her plan worked, Mary-Kate's name would be cleared by this time tomorrow.

Just in time for the festival!

CHAPTER ELEVEN

"Mary-Kate Burke? Can you tell the class what colour rose symbolized the House of Lancaster in their war against the House of York?"

Mary-Kate's head snapped up. Mr Yoshida was staring at her, his arms crossed over his chest. *Uh-oh*, Mary-Kate thought. *Do I know the answer to this?*

"I'm waiting, Ms Burke," he said patiently.

Mary-Kate shuffled frantically through her history notes. The problem was, she had only half of them. The other half was in Gomez's stomach!

"Colour, colour," Mary-Kate muttered as she continued to shuffle. "Purple? Magenta? Electric-green? Gold glitter?"

"Ms Burke? May I inquire as to what happened

to your notes?" Mr Yoshida asked her.

Mary-Kate blushed. "Uh . . . a goat ate them."

Everyone in the class cracked up.

"A goat ate them," Mr Yoshida said, frowning. "That's very original. Next time, please be better prepared."

He glanced round the classroom. "Does anyone know the answer?"

Hans raised his hand. "The emblem of the House of Lancaster was a red rose."

"Very good, Mr Jensen," Mr Yoshida said, beaming. "I see no goats have been eating *your* notes."

There were several sniggers. Mary-Kate glared at Hans. He gave her a superior-looking smile.

Just wait until my sister gets the real goat thief, Mary-Kate thought. *I'll show you!*

Mary-Kate could barely concentrate through the rest of Mr Yoshida's lecture. As soon as class was over, she gathered up her stuff and rushed up to Ashley.

"Okay, you said yesterday that you had a plan to catch the goat thief after our history lesson," Mary-Kate whispered. "It's after class now. So what's the plan?"

"We have to get to work before everyone packs

up their notebooks," Ashley whispered back.
"Whoever has the stationery with the asteroids and
stuff on it is our goat thief! You take the right half of
the room, and I'll take the left!"

"Got it!" Mary-Kate said.

Out of the corner of her eye, Mary-Kate saw that
Dana was packing up her stuff. Mary-Kate made a
beeline for Dana's desk.

Dana gave her a frosty look. "Yes?" she said.
"What may I do for you?"

Mary-Kate saw that Dana had closed her
notebook. "I was wondering if I could borrow a
piece of paper."

"What's wrong with *your* notebook?" Dana
asked her suspiciously. "Did Gomez eat it?"

"Yeah, Dana, ha ha," Mary-Kate said. "Actually,
um, I ran out of paper. Mr Yoshida's lecture was so
interesting, I took a lot of notes."

Dana sighed, then opened her notebook and
ripped out a page. "Here you go," she said, handing
it to Mary-Kate.

Mary-Kate studied it. It had exotic-looking
butterflies all along the border of it. No black stars,
no asteroids, no spaceships.

Does that mean Dana didn't steal Gomez? Mary-
Kate wondered. *Or does she have other notepaper, too?*

Just then, she noticed Ashley frantically waving her arms in the air. She was standing just behind Arthur Nunzio, whose desk was across from his brother Andrew's. The two boys were packing up their stuff and didn't seem to notice Ashley standing there.

I wonder what's up? Mary-Kate thought, rushing over.

Ashley stabbed a finger towards Arthur's desk.

Mary-Kate's eyes followed Ashley's finger. Arthur's notebook was lying on his desk. It was open at the first page – which had black stars, asteroids, and spaceships on it!

And across from him, his twin brother Andrew was pulling a purple magic marker out of his backpack!

"*You* two are the goat thieves!" Mary-Kate cried out.

"We caught you red-handed!" Ashley declared.

Everyone in the class stopped talking. Mr Yoshida came over. "What's going on?" he demanded.

Arthur and Andrew turned red. *They're guilty!* Mary-Kate thought gleefully.

"Uh, we, uh, d-don't know what these girls are t-talking about, Mr Yoshida," Arthur sputtered.

"Yeah, we're innocent!" Andrew added. He

glared at Mary-Kate and Ashley and said, "You can't go around accusing people without any proof!"

You want proof? Mary-Kate thought. She reached into her pocket and pulled out the crumpled-up piece of paper with the words "PORTER 12" on it.

"We found this in my room," she told Mr Yoshida. "Whoever planted Gomez the Goat in my room dropped it on my floor. The stationery matches Arthur's, and the pen matches Andrew's!"

Take that, Nunzios! Mary-Kate thought triumphantly.

Arthur and Andrew gaped at the piece of paper. Their faces were even redder than before. Mr Yoshida stared at them, and said, "Arthur. Andrew. What do you have to say for yourselves?"

"It wasn't my idea," Arthur whined. He pointed at his brother. "It was his."

"I don't think so," Andrew shot back. "Who was the one who said Mary-Kate was a menace to the Harrington team and had to be taken out?"

"And who suggested planting Gomez in her room?" Arthur returned.

Mary-Kate turned to Mr Yoshida. "Now we know who stole the goat. Why don't you ask them if they took the trophy and put acorns on the pizzas, too?" The two brothers glared at each other.

I'm going to ask them a lot of questions." Mr Yoshida looked stern. "We're going to the Headmaster's office. *Now!*"

"Yes, Mr Yoshida," Arthur and Andrew mumbled in unison.

After they left, Ashley started jumping up and down. "Yeah! We did it, Mary-Kate!" she crowed.

"*You* did it, Ashley!" Mary-Kate told her, hugging her gratefully. "Your plan worked!"

Phoebe and Wendy rushed over to Mary-Kate and Ashley. "What's going on? What happened?"

Ashley told them the whole story. While they were talking, Campbell came up to Mary-Kate. "Way to go, MK!" she said, slapping Mary-Kate on the back.

Mary-Kate felt like jumping up and down and screaming. *I'm free!* she thought. *I'm back in the Winter Festival! I'm—*

Totally out of shape!

"Campbell?" she said in a small voice. "I don't know if I can do this."

"Do what, MK?" Campbell asked her.

"Participate in the Winter Festival," Mary-Kate explained. "I mean, I haven't been at any of the practices in almost a week! And the Winter Festival is three days away! How am I supposed to compete in downhill skiing, cross-country, skating and snowboarding when all I've been doing for the last six days is—"

"Mary-Kate?"

Mary-Kate felt someone tapping her on the shoulder. She turned round. It was Lexy Martin.

"Um, I have some bad news for you," Lexy said. "We kind of had to fill your spot on the downhill team. So we won't be needing you any more."

"Oh," Mary-Kate said, taken aback.

Then Fiona Ferris came up to her. "Ditto with the snowboarding team," Fiona said apologetically. "We had to fill your slot, because we didn't think you were coming back. Sorry!"

"Oh," Mary-Kate said. *Now, it's down to two teams*, she thought.

Just then, she saw Lisa Dunmead heading in her direction. Before Lisa had a chance to speak, Mary-Kate said, "I know. I'm off the skating team, right?"

"How did you know?" Lisa asked her, looking surprised.

Mary-Kate shrugged. "Wild guess."

As Lisa turned to go, Mary-Kate sighed. *I'm kind of disappointed, but I'm kind of relieved, too*, she thought. *I mean, four teams are way too many for me to handle at this point.*

"MK?"

Campbell was grinning at her. "*We* still want you. The cross-country-skiing team, I mean."

"You do?" Mary-Kate said, surprised. "You didn't kick me off, too?"

Campbell shook her head. "Amy Martinez has been filling in for you, but she really doesn't want to race if she doesn't have to."

Mary-Kate thought long and hard. *Can I do this?* she wondered. *Can I really get back in super-athlete shape in just three days – and lead the cross-country-skiing team to victory?*

Yes, I can!

CHAPTER TWELVE

It was the morning of the Winter Festival. Ashley was putting the finishing touches on her snow supermodel for the snow sculpture contest. It was dressed in snow capri pants, a snow tank top and snow platform shoes.

Ashley stepped back and looked at her creation. *The face is kind of lumpy,* she thought. *But I still think everyone can tell it's a girl!*

The White Oak campus was a madhouse. White Oak and Harrington students and teachers were running around everywhere, getting ready for the competitions.

Everything's been going so well these last few days, Ashley thought. *We caught the real goat thieves. The pep rally was a big success. So was the cake sale – we raised lots of money for the hats!*

Just then, one of Ashley's snow supermodel's ears fell off. Ashley frowned, and stuck it back on. *Speaking of hats, where's Phoebe?* she wondered. *She was supposed to be here with the hats an hour ago.*

"Ashley!" a familiar voice yelled. Phoebe was running across the courtyard. "We have an emergency!" She skidded to a stop in front of Ashley, panting.

"Phoebe, what's up?" Ashley asked her. She hadn't seen her roommate this upset since they'd cancelled her favourite show on cable, *Oldies but Goodies*, all about vintage clothes.

"My beautiful, wonderful, designer Winter Festival hats have been stolen!" Phoebe cried out.

Ashley couldn't believe her ears. "What?"

"I'm telling you, someone stole all the hats!" Phoebe moaned.

"How do you know someone stole them?" Ashley asked her. "Maybe they just got moved or something."

Phoebe shook her head. "No, they were definitely stolen. I checked on them last night. They were in the cupboard next to Ms Bloomberg's classroom. And when Wendy and I went to get them an hour ago, they were gone! Missing! Vanished without a trace!"

This is not good, Ashley thought. And then an idea came to her. "The boys! Maybe it was the Harrington boys!"

Phoebe looked puzzled. "But the Nunzio twins have been caught. Weren't they responsible for all the shenanigans?"

Ashley shook her head. "Sure, Arthur and Andrew stole the trophy and put acorns on the pizza. But Dana and Kristin admitted they painted a rat on the Harrington sign."

"Dana and Kristin wouldn't steal our hats," Phoebe argued. She thought for a moment. "Would they?"

"Hey, Lexy! Hey, Lisa! You guys need a Winter Festival hat?"

Ashley whirled around at the sound of the familiar voice. *Dana!*

Dana, Kristin and Summer were walking around with big cardboard boxes. They were distributing Winter Festival hats to Lexy and Lisa and a bunch of other White Oak girls.

Ashley and Phoebe rushed up to them. "What are you doing with the hats, Dana?" Ashley demanded.

"I made an executive decision last night," Dana

announced smoothly. "These hats needed a little . . . *retouching.*"

"*What?*" Phoebe gasped.

Ashley glared at Dana, then grabbed a hat out of one of the boxes. And studied it carefully.

It's the same green fleece cap as before, Ashley thought, relieved. *It's the same squirrel, too . . . with earmuffs and a muffler and skates – and a sword!*

The squirrel was holding a sword in its hand, as if it were going to battle!

Phoebe's going to be so upset! Ashley thought.

But to Ashley's total surprise, Phoebe had a smile on her face. "It's a bold concept," she said to Dana. "I like it! It's a clever cross between the White Oak mascot motif and the battle motif! Very New England boarding school meets Cartoon Channel meets Trojan War!"

"Thank you, Phoebe," Dana said.

"Seriously cool," Lexy agreed, putting on her hat.

Lisa put hers on, too. "Yeah. Way to go, School Spirit Committee!"

Ashley sighed. She had to admit, the hats *did* look kind of cute. "Yeah, they are nice," she said to Dana. "But why didn't you ask us?"

Just then, a voice came over the loudspeakers.

"It's time for the athletic competitions to begin. Everyone please come to the main gate for the opening ceremonies!"

Ashley grabbed Phoebe's arm. "Let's go," she urged. "Mary-Kate's about to start her race!"

CHAPTER THIRTEEN

Mary-Kate, Campbell and their two cross-country team-mates were in a huddle at the starting line.

"Okay," Campbell was saying to Mary-Kate and the other girls. "Let's review this. Hans, Ross and the other Harrington guys skied this course in twenty-eight minutes and twenty seconds."

That's a really good time, Mary-Kate thought nervously.

She had been practising superhard since Tuesday, to catch up on her six days of no practice at all.

But is it going to be enough? Mary-Kate wondered. *Am I going to be able to come through for my team – and for all the White Oak students?*

The skating, snowboarding and downhill-skiing competitions had already taken place. Harrington had won the downhill-skiing competition, and White Oak had taken skating. They had tied on snowboarding.

Which means that cross-country is going to be the tiebreaker, she thought.

"We can do this!" Campbell said.

That's it, Mary-Kate thought. *Positive attitude!*

"We're warriors!" Mary-Kate said, raising her fist in the air. But she didn't feel as confident as she sounded.

The four team-mates exchanged high-fives, then split up to take their positions on the circular trail. Mary-Kate snapped on her skis and started skiing into the woods. Behind her, she could see Ashley jumping up and down, cheering her on. Mary-Kate waved back to her. She tried not to look nervous, even though she had a zillion butterflies in her stomach.

Mary-Kate finally reached her position on the trail. A few minutes later, she could hear the starting gun going off, and the sounds of the crowd shouting and cheering.

In just twenty minutes the first three girls will have finished skiing their legs, she thought. *And then – it will be my turn!*

While she waited, Mary-Kate skied round in circles to keep herself warm. She did leg stretches. She took lots of deep breaths to try to make the butterflies go away.

She kept telling herself over and over again: *I can do it. I can do it. I can do it.*

In what seemed like no time at all, she saw Campbell skiing towards her. Two judges skied right behind her, to make sure she stayed on the path.

"MK!" Campbell yelled breathlessly as she came skiing up the hilly path toward Mary-Kate. Campbell stumbled a little, reached out, and slapped Mary-Kate's hand. "Go, go, *go!*"

Mary-Kate dug her poles into the deep snow and plunged ahead. The butterflies were gone. She was completely focused on the path, on the motion of her arms and legs. Her skis made a soft *swooshing* noise as they glided across the snow.

It was hard to believe that two *weeks* ago she hadn't known how to cross-country ski. Now she felt as though she had been doing this all her life.

She skied ahead at an impossible speed, kicking white powder everywhere around her. Her muscles ached, but she didn't care. She pushed herself harder than she had ever pushed herself before.

Before long, the finishing line came into view. There was a huge crowd standing there. Ashley, Phoebe, Wendy and Campbell were jumping up and down and screaming. Hans Jensen was there, too, along with several other boys from Harrington. Hans kept looking nervously at Mary-Kate, then at his watch.

Mary-Kate had no idea how close her team's time was to the Harrington team's time. *But from the way Hans is acting, it must be close*, she thought excitedly.

She had no more energy left in her muscles, and no more air left in her lungs. But she pushed herself into overdrive, anyway. She skied the last fifty feet of the path like a total maniac.

She crossed the finishing line.

One of the judges peered at her watch. "The official time is . . . twenty-eight minutes and ten seconds!" she announced. "White Oak wins by ten seconds. Which means that White Oak wins the Winter Festival trophy!"

All the girls in the crowd went wild. Campbell ran over to Mary-Kate and engulfed her in a bear hug. Ashley came rushing up to them and gave them *both* hugs.

"Way to go, MK!" Campbell shouted.

"Way to go, sis!" Ashley shouted. "We're so proud of you!"

Out of the corner of her eye, Mary-Kate saw Hans Jensen coming up to her. *What's the right thing to say here?* she wondered. *Ha, ha, Hans? Got you?*

But before she had a chance to say anything, Hans held out his hand. "Congratulations," he said simply. "You skied really well."

Mary-Kate was totally awestruck. "Uh, thanks," she said after a moment. "You skied really well, too."

"Of course, I'll beat you next year," Hans added.

Mary-Kate laughed. *This* was the Hans she was used to. "In your dreams!" she told him.

Ashley tugged on Mary-Kate's arm. "Come on, Mary-Kate. Let's go to the awards ceremony. It's trophy time!"

"And then there's a big pizza celebration party in the dining hall," Campbell said.

Mary-Kate grinned. "Pizza? With or without acorns?"

ACORN

The Voice of White Oak Academy Since 1905

THAW-ABLE ART
by Phoebe Cahill

The White Oak/Harrington Winter Festival was about more than just sports. It was all about snow. Twenty contestants packed, moulded, and carved a whole lotta snow for the Snow Sculpture Contest. The results were totally cool (I mean cold).

It was a nail-biting finish as the judges agonized over their decisions. The winners were announced – and the crowd was on its feet!

First place went to First Former John McCall, creator of an elaborate snow Statue of Liberty. Fiona Ferris won a second place medal for her life-size snow sculpture of Mrs P holding a bowl of snow oatmeal. And third place went to the *Acorn*'s own

Ashley Burke, who created a snow supermodel dressed in the latest resort wear: snow capri pants, snow tank top and snow platform shoes. (What, Ashley, no snowglasses?)

GLAM GAB
by Ashley Burke and Phoebe Cahill

Fashion expert Ashley Burke

You're dying for a Whole New Look, but your wardrobe budget is like the weather – below zero! The good news is, there are ways to spruce up your style without breaking the bank. Here are a few of our favourites:

•**The Power of One**. Consider buying just ONE new item of clothing to wear with a lot of things. Think black cable-knit sweater, think great-fitting jeans, think supercool boots. One new "classic" can go a long way to liven up your wardrobe.

•**One Girl's Trash Is Another Girl's Treasure**. If you have a friend or room-

mate who wears the same size as you, why not swap? She may adore your tired old pink cashmere sweater, and that black spandex dress she's worn a zillion times may be just what you need. Remember, it's nice to share!

•**Go Vintage!** Vintage clothing stores, garage sales and flea markets can be terrific sources of cheap, cool clothes and accessories. Some recent finds: A pair of 1970s bell bottoms with a peace-sign patch for 50

cents; a hot-pink fake-fur jacket for $5.

•**When in Doubt, Accessorize!** Accessories can make a yawner outfit look brand-new for almost no money at all. Make a statement with a hat, a scarf, a belt. And don't forget about hair accessories like hair clips, slides and scrunchies!

RIVALRY ON ICE!
White Oak and Harrington Hit the Pond in First-Ever Figure-Skating Event
by Mary-Kate Burke

Figure skating was added to the Winter Festival line-up for the first time this year.

Sports pro Mary-Kate Burke

Sarah Cooper, who performed her routine to a disco version of "Winter Wonderland" sung by chipmunks, won major points for her double axel. But Hans Jensen pulled off an awesome double lutz, which gave Harrington the edge going into the second half of the event.

A near-tragedy happened when Lisa Dunmead was distracted by a stray dog while doing a backward

figure-eight. She skidded into Bob the caretaker, who was chasing the dog. Fortunately, Lisa recovered her balance and finished the rest of her routine like a pro. And the dog has found a happy home – with Bob!

In the end, victory proved slippery for both White Oak and Harrington and the two schools finished in a tie.

Due to the popularity of the figure-skating event, speed-skating may be added to NEXT year's Winter Festival. Better start doing those quadricep exercises now, White Oakers!

THE GET-REAL GIRL

Dear Get-Real Girl:
Help! I have a crush on *two* Harrington guys, and I can't decide which one to ask to the Sadie Hawkins Dance next month. One of them, HJ, is seriously cute.

But whenever we hang out, the only thing we talk about is HIM. The other guy, SW, looks like Bart Simpson on a bad hair day. But he's got a great sense of humour, and he's really sweet. What should I do?

Signed,
Torn

Dear Torn:
It's simple. Do you want to spend the evening looking at HJ looking at himself in the mirror? Or do you want to spend it looking at SW looking at YOU? Unless

you want to play one-girl fan club to Mr I'm-So-Hot, my advice is: Go to the dance with SW! If things work out, you can always buy him some hair gel for Valentine's Day!

Signed,
Get-Real Girl

Dear Get-Real Girl:
My birthday's coming up, and I want to have a skating party. The problem is, two of my best mates, "N" and "P," can't stand each other. I want to invite

them both, but I know that's just asking for trouble. What should I do?
Signed,
Caught in the Middle

Dear Caught in the Middle:
"N" and "P" need to understand something. It's YOUR birthday! On your big day, everyone has to cater to you totally and completely. That means not letting petty personal grudges spoil the fun. So when you email the invites, add a P.S. to "N" and "P" telling them to leave their attitudes at the door. And if they can't, that should tell YOU something: it's time to find a couple of new friends!
Signed,
Get-Real Girl

THE FIRST FORM BUZZ
By Dana Woletsky

It's Cabin Fever time, because let's face it: who wants to ruin their brand-new Italian suede boots in the snow? But there are advantages to being stuck inside. Like, a person can overhear a lot of gossip in the hallways, in the common room, and at the pay phone . . .

For example! WHO KEEPS STEALING ALL THE PURPLE SOCKS FROM THE PHIPPS HOUSE LAUNDRY ROOM? There is a mysterious sock thief on the loose. Her M.O.: she sneaks in during the spin cycle and steals only purple socks. Three Phipps

First Formers have reported missing socks.

Will this very strange mystery be solved? Stay tuned!

Was Gomez the Goat REALLY planted in the room of a certain Porter House resident with the initials MKB? Rumour has

it that a couple of Harrington twins took the fall for Gomez's goat-napping to cover up for MKB. She actually wanted him for a pet! If MKB wanted to violate the "No Pets at White Oak" rule, she should have gone for something easier to hide – like a hamster!

Good news! The pre-Winter Festival cake sale was a huge success, and raised enough money to

pay for the excellent Winter Festival hats – designed by me! Many thanks to the School Spirit Committee – chaired by me – for organizing the sale!

That's all for now. And don't forget! Keep School Spirit going year-round by emailing any and all hot gossip to me c/o The Buzz Girl at the *Acorn*!

UPCOMING CALENDAR

•Got the January blues? On January 24th, Porter House will be transformed into Porter-Rico for the

annual Tropical Paradise Party. Come in your bathing suits, shorts, halter tops and hula skirts. The thermostat will be cranked up high, and the pineapple punch will be flowing!

•There will be no classes on Presidents' Day! Honour our nation's presidents by remembering their achievements – and sleeping in late!

•Attention, future Picassos! Entries are now being

accepted for the annual White Oak student art show. Paintings, photographs, oatmeal sculptures, whatever – YOU'RE the artist.

•Who says guys can't boil water? On April 4, Harrington will hold its annual Pizza Bake-Off. There will be three award categories: Best Tasting, Most Original Recipe and

Most Likely to Cause Heartburn. So bring your appetites and Alka-Seltzer and get chewing!

•Spring is just around the corner! The Spring Fling dance will be on April 18. Think cool music, warm breezes and hot guys. Not to mention an excuse to buy a spring-y new dress. Who could ask for more?

Winter Horoscopes

Aquarius:
(January 20–February 18)

Water-bearers are great visionaries, and they want to shower the world with their brilliant ideas. But you've got plenty of time to solve the global-warming problem or come up with a cure for cancer. Right now, enjoy being a student. That means reading and learning. And, of course, giving yourself avocado facials, eating pizza and hanging out with your mates!

Pisces:
(February 19–March 20)

Hey, Pisces! You tend to feel like a fish out of water when you aren't helping other people. You're always there when your best friend wants to gab about her guy troubles, or when your roommate needs tutoring for the History test. But it's important to think about YOURSELF once in a while. So do something just for you: re-read a favourite book, take a walk, or head for the shops.

Aries:
(March 21–April 19)

Aries girls are always the leaders of the pack. You're energetic, you're dynamic, you get things going. Bottom line: you rule! The problem is, you have a tendency to ram ideas down people's throats. The next time you're in charge of a project try sitting back and letting others do the talking. It's a lot easier to get your herd to follow you if you let them know their contributions matter!

PSST! Take a sneak peek at

Likes Me, Likes Me Not!

Mary-Kate ran out of her room. Her heart was pounding and her face was burning hot.

How could she? How could Campbell betray me like this? Mary-Kate wondered. *How could she go out with the boy I like?*

She dashed out of Porter House and along the walkway leading to Phipps.

I don't even know which room she's in! she realized as she yanked open the other dorm's front door.

Inside, just off the lobby, a bunch of girls were gathered in the common room. Mary-Kate poked her head in.

"Uh, does anyone know which room Campbell Smith has?" she asked. "She's just swapped with Ginger Halliday. Jamie Randoph is her roommate."

"Upstairs. First door on the left," a girl said.

"Thanks," Mary-Kate said.

Her throat started to tighten as she took the stairs two at a time.

What if she's not there? What if she's out for a walk or something?

Or what if she's on the hall phone right now – talking to him? To Grant?

Mary-Kate got madder and madder with every step.

By the time she reached Campbell's new room, she felt like her blood was boiling!

Campbell was sprawled on a rug on the floor, reading her book for English.

"Hello, traitor!" Mary-Kate snapped. She stood in the doorway with her hands on her hips.

Campbell's head shot up with a jerk. "Uh, hi. What's wrong with you?"

"Oh, nothing," Mary-Kate said, sounding hurt and angry at the same time. "I just can't believe you've stolen the only guy I really liked – that's all!"

"What are you talking about?" Campbell asked. She dropped her book and sat up, cross-legged. She really did look puzzled.

"Don't play dumb," Mary-Kate cried. "I'm talking about Grant! You're going to the dance with him!"

Then she realized she was almost yelling. She checked over her shoulder to see if anyone had heard her in the hall. The coast was clear. "How could you?" she asked more softly.

"Why shouldn't I go with Grant?" Campbell answered. "You said you never wanted to hear his name again!"

I did? When? Mary-Kate thought. *Oh, yeah. In the dining hall.*

But that was only because . . . because everyone was driving her crazy!

Mary-Kate felt like she was going to cry. She didn't want Campbell to see.

"I'm just saying, that's not how roommates treat each other," Mary-Kate shot back. Her voice was still shaky. "Not if they're really friends."

Then she spun around and stormed out.

Her heart was still pounding as she started down the front steps.

A gang of girls were coming up.

Oh, no, Mary-Kate thought. *They're going to see that I'm almost crying.*

She turned round and ran back down the hall, past Campbell's room.

I'll take the back staircase, she thought. But the last room on the right, near the stairs, was brightly lit.

Mary-Kate could hear voices inside, talking. Even before she got there, she recognized one of the voices. It was Dana Woletsky.

You could tell her voice anywhere, Mary-Kate thought. She always sounded so snooty and stuck-up.

"So I just figured, why wait for him to ask me?" Dana was saying. "So I asked him to the dance!"

"And he said yes?" another girl in the room asked.

"Yup. I'm going to the Spring Fling with Ross!" Dana announced.

Ross? Ross Lambert? But that was the guy Ashley wanted to go with!

Oh, no! Mary-Kate thought. *This is the worst!*

She wanted to crawl under a radiator and hide.

She and Ashley had both been dumped by the guys they liked!

mary-kateandashley

TWO of a kind ™

Coming soon – can you collect them all?

HarperCollins*Entertainment*

PARACHUTE PRESS

DUALSTAR PUBLICATIONS

mary-kateandashley.com
AOL Keyword: mary-kateandashley

mary-kateandashley

Meet Chloe and Riley Carlson.
So much to do...

so little time

HarperCollins*Entertainment*

 PARACHUTE PRESS

 DUALSTAR PUBLICATIONS

 mary-kateandashley.com
AOL Keyword: mary-kateandashley

TM & © 2002 Dualstar Entertainment Group, LLC.

Mary-Kate and Ashley in their latest movie adventure

Passport to Paris

Available on video from 11th March

 mary-kateandashley.com AOL Keyword: mary-kateandashley DUALSTAR VIDEO

Get ready to celebrate with the Real Dolls for Real Girls

Mary-Kate & Ashley Birthday Bash Fashion Dolls!

Celebrate with birthday cake, present, and a camera to capture the memories!

Plus a hip floral halter dress included for trendy birthday style!

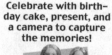

DUALSTAR CONSUMER PRODUCTS

mary-kateandashley AOL mary-kateandashley.com AOL Keyword: mary-kateandashley

Mary-Kate and Ashley's latest exciting movie adventure

Available to own on video and DVD 29th July 2002

DUALSTAR VIDEO

mary-kateandashley.com
AOL Keyword: mary-kateandashley

It's What YOU Watch!

Mary-Kate and Ashley Sweet 16

PlayStation.2

GAME BOY ADVANCE

NINTENDO GAMECUBE

DUALSTAR INTERACTIVE

Games for Girls.

mary-kateandashley.com
AOL Keyword: mary-kateandashley

CLUB Acclaim

Order Form

To order direct from the publishers, just make a list of the titles you want and fill in the form below:

Name ....

Address ....

....

....

Send to: Dept 6, HarperCollins Publishers Ltd, Westerhill Road, Bishopbriggs, Glasgow G64 2QT.

Please enclose a cheque or postal order to the value of the cover price, plus:

UK & BFPO: Add £1.00 for the first book, and 25p per copy for each additional book ordered.

Overseas and Eire: Add £2.95 service charge. Books will be sent by surface mail but quotes for airmail despatch will be given on request.

A 24-hour telephone ordering service is available to holders of Visa, MasterCard, Amex or Switch cards on 0141- 772 2281.

An imprint of HarperCollins*Publishers*